Opa and Me

Written by Kevin M. Donovan
Illustrated by Mariana Dragomirova

D1404525

ISBN 978-1-61225-191-2

©Copyright 2012 Kevin M. Donovan
All rights reserved

No part of this publication may be reproduced in any form or stored, transmitted or recorded by any means without the written permission of the author.

Published by Mirror Publishing
Milwaukee, WI 53214

Printed in the USA.

For Helga: my best friend, my inspiration,
my wife

I have an Opa.
I love him lots.

I have my hat. He has his Hut.
I ask him how he's been. "Oh Schatz, sehr gut."

I love the snow,
I have to say.

Opa walks slow,
Just like me.

We take time to talk.
We take time to see.

When I walk with Opa,
I learn something new.
Like Hund and Katze,
And a German song or two.

A tree is a Baum,
And a river a Fluss.

Opa tries to teach me German,
A new word every day.
Today the word is weiss.
The color of the Schnee.

As we walk through the woods,
It's a wintery cold.

I start to shake and shiver,
Until I have a warm hand to hold.

Opa starts to sing.
That always makes me smile.

We stop on the Brücke.
And we stand for a while.

We just stand there and listen.
We hear everything.
The frozen trees creaking,
And a bird starts to sing.

I would like to speak German.
But I've never dared.
I'm always too shy.
I'm always too scared.

As we start walking again,
I'm determined to try.
The words almost come out,
But then I just sigh.

Opa and me.
Opa und ich.
"Oh Opa..."

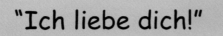
"Ich liebe dich!"

Opa and Me
What the German words mean

Baum = tree

Brücke = bridge

Fluss = river

Hund = dog

Hut = hat

Ich liebe den Schnee = I love the snow

Ich liebe dich = I love you

Katze = cat

Opa = grandfather

Opa und ich = Opa and me

Schatz = sweetheart

Schnee = snow

sehr gut = very good

weiss = white

Wir gehen zu Fuss = We go for a walk

CPSIA information can be obtained
at www.ICGtesting.com
Printed in the USA
BVIC01n1207090214
344339BV00002B/3

9 781612 251912